Little Dreamer, Ignite!

Written by **Jaime Grace**

Illustrated by Charity Wittenbach

WestBow Press books may be ordered through booksellers or by contacting:

WestBow Press
A Division of Thomas Nelson & Zondervan
1663 Liberty Drive
Bloomington, IN 47403
www.westbowpress.com
844-714-3454

Interior Image Credit: Charity Wittenbach

ISBN: 978-1-6642-4774-1 (sc)
ISBN: 978-1-6642-4775-8 (hc)
ISBN: 978-1-6642-4773-4 (e)

Library of Congress Control Number: 2021921498

Print information available on the last page.

WestBow Press rev. date: 12/1/2021

Little Dreamer, Ignite!

Jeremiah 1:5 NIV
"Before I formed you in the womb I knew you,
before you were born I set you apart."

Dedicated to Abba Father, who has called me by name
and ignited my spirit, soul, and body to life.

To my God-given Mom and Dad who saw in me the promises from
above and ignited in me hidden treasures I never knew existed.

Special thanks to Charity Wittenbach for your beautiful heart and artwork; I have been incredibly
blessed to walk through this with you. To my Mom and editor; for your wisdom, expertise, and
your continual guidance and encouragement, I cannot thank you enough for the countless times
you have poured into my life. Jade Jeffries, I am so grateful for your love of the written word. To all
who have prayed and encouraged me along the way, thank you. I am incredibly blessed that my
Father desired for each of you to be in my life and a part of the story he is so beautifully writing.

Isaiah 45:3 NIV

"I will give you hidden treasures, riches stored in secret places, so that you may
know that I am the LORD, the God of Israel, who summons you by name"

Contents

To All Who Love Little Dreamers

Who am I? Who has God created me to be?

Deep within my own heart I have pondered those very questions. I was recently sitting by a stunning mountain stream taking in the sounds, smells, and views which surrounded me in every direction, when I began to sense the vastness, and depth of the Father's endless love for each one of us. As His presence weighed heavy on my heart I felt His deep desire to reveal the very unique and perfectly exquisite treasures that are hidden deep within each one us. An invitation to walk with Him into deeper revelation of who He has created us to be through our giftings, passions, talents, etc. which are like tiny embers waiting to be ignited and fanned into flames.

From that very moment we could understand the meaning of purpose, we have longed to know ours. Who am I? Who has God created me to be? And I truly believe that it is one of God's deepest desires for you to know who you are in Him! The beautiful treasures He has put in you are a part of the adventure He desires to join you, in unwrapping.

Parents, Grandparents, and all of you who love the Little Dreamers, possess the precious gift and privilege of partnering with God and lovingly guiding them to seek out the hidden treasures in your beautifully created little masterpieces. And today we can help them begin forming dreams for their futures.

I invite you to accompany me on this beauty filled treasure hunt through the pages of this book with your Little Dreamer snuggled in close, to discover the hidden treasures deep within their little hearts, and yours also. Page by page, may adventure after adventure open up to you and your little one as together we explore the heart of the Father and His perfect and unique one-of-a-kind YOU!

In this book you will find:

- Stories to help you and your little dreamer identify and ignite treasures God has planted within
- Questions to talk through together as your Little Dreamer starts to dream
- Names of God and their significance
- An index of qualities often associated with various careers and callings
- Journaling pages for recording discoveries, inspirations, ideas, and prayers
- A prayer to pray over your Little Dreamer
- And more

May you be richly blessed as you discover how intimately loved and wonderfully designed each Little Dreamer is.

With much grace,
Jaime

Little Musician, Ignite!

Little Ace and Ariella love playing and singing with Mommy and Daddy in their family's band, The Little Rockers. They all play and sing because their hearts are full of joy. Sometimes Ace and Ariella get to play in children's church with all the other kids. After they have practiced and practiced, they sometimes even get to sing and play for the grownups! During the worship you can hear the flute, tambourine, trumpet, harmonica, and the sound of happy voices filling the air.

Psalm 100:1-3 NIV

"Shout for joy to the LORD, all the earth. Worship the LORD with gladness; come before him with joyful songs. Know that the LORD is God. It is he, who made us, and we are his; we are his people, the sheep of his pasture."

Immanuel-"God With Us."

Little Dreamer, Ignite!

Can you find the hidden dove in the picture?

What is your favorite musical instrument to listen to? Would you like to learn to play an instrument?

Can you sing your favorite song right now, or make up a brand new song of your own?

How can you share music with others?

How would you like to thank God for music and singing?

Little Doctor, Ignite!

Little Ryder and Gracie's aunt and uncle are doctors at the hospital near their house. Sometimes Ryder and Gracie go to the hospital with Aunt Abigail and Uncle Jake to visit little boys and girls who are not feeling well. Gracie likes to listen to the heartbeats and Ryder likes to check their temperature. Sometimes they get to color pictures and read books with the patients too, which makes everyone feel better!

Jeremiah 17:14 NIV
"Heal me, LORD, and I will be healed; save me and I will be saved, for you are the one I praise."

Jehovah Rapha–"God Who Heals."

Little Dreamer, Ignite!

Can you find the dove in the picture?
How can you help others when they are not feeling well?
Who helps you feel better when you're sick or hurt?
How do you feel when you are sick?
Would you like to thank God for your good health?

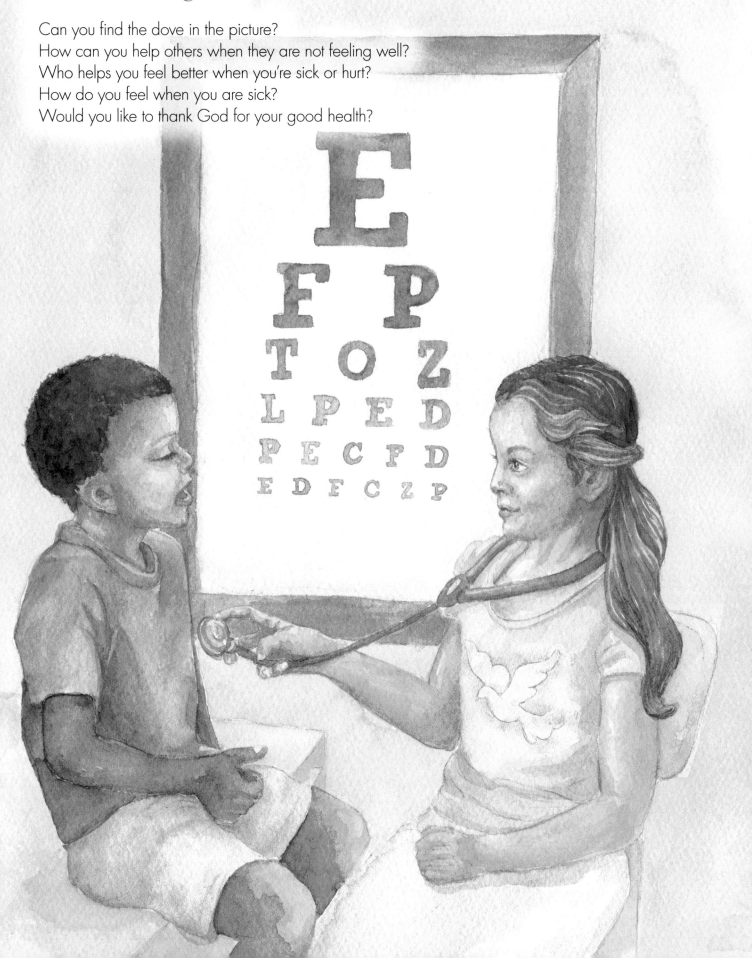

Little Teacher, Ignite!

Little Noah and his sister Ava are so excited! Today is a very special day for them at school. Their art teacher, Miss Andrea, has asked Ava and Noah to do what they love best: teaching their classmates how to draw animals. The students have been learning all about elephants, giraffes, lions, and rhinos, and today they're going to create a huge, colorful mural of an African safari. Noah and Ava are so happy when teaching others how to draw and paint animals.

Psalm 78:1 NIV

"My people hear my teaching; listen
to the words of my mouth."

Rabbi –"Teacher."

Little Dreamer, Ignite!

Can you find the hidden dove in the picture?
Have you helped someone learn something new?
Who helps you learn new things?
What do you like to learn about?
Would you like to thank God for the people who help
you learn new things?

Little Dancer, Ignite!

Little Beau and Piper are dressed and ready to go on stage at the Dreamers Dance Company. They are ready to dance to the song, "This Little Light of Mine." Beau is looking very handsome in his black and white suit and shiny black shoes. Piper feels beautiful in her pink dress and best dance shoes. Piper and Beau's friends and family are all here watching them dance, and the children couldn't be happier.

2 Samuel 6:14 NIV
"David was dancing before the Lord with all his might."

Jehovah Nissi –"The Lord My Banner."

Little Dreamer, Ignite!

Can you find the hidden dove in the picture?
When you dance, do you like others to watch, or do you prefer dancing by yourself? Why?
Would you like to dance right now? Let's do it together!
Have you ever danced on a stage? How did it make you feel when people clapped for you?
Would you like to thank God for dancing?

Little Officer, Ignite!

Little Gabriel and Madeline are dressed and waiting for Grandma and Grandpa to pick them up for a special date! They're all going to ride in a police car with two police officers that protect their community. What fun it's going to be to turn on the loud siren and bright lights, lighting up the night sky with red, white, and blue.

Isaiah 41:10 NASB

'Do not fear, for I am with you; Do not be afraid, for I am your God. I will strengthen you, I will also help you, I will also uphold you with My righteous right hand.

'Jehovah-Roi –"The Lord My Protector."

Little Dreamer, Ignite!

Can you find the hidden dove in the picture?
Do you know how officers protect you and the people in your community?
Who else protects you?
Have you ever helped or protected someone you care about?
Would you like to thank God for keeping you safe and protected at all times?

Little Astronaut, Ignite!

Little Cross and Lily are ready to enter their rocket, "Little Dreamer." It's time to launch! They can't wait to fly up above the earth's atmosphere to see all the wonders God has created-planets, the moon, stars, asteroids, comets, nebulas, and galaxies. What a great adventure it's going to be!

Nehemiah 9:6 NLT

"You alone are the LORD. You made the skies and the heavens and all the stars. You made the earth and the seas and everything in them. You preserve them all, and the angels of heaven worship you."

El Elyon –"The Most High God."

Little Dreamer, Ignite!

Can you find the hidden dove in the picture?
What is one of the greatest adventures you have had?
Can you think of an adventure you would like to go on someday?
How can you prepare for a great adventure?
Would you like to thank God for the exciting places you've gotten to visit?

Little Lawyer, Ignite!

Little Cade and Eden love to act just like real lawyers and help people who are not being treated kindly or need help to make better decisions. Today, they are helping Joshua. Joshua is sad because a boy bullied him in his neighborhood. Cade and Eden talked to the bully and helped him understand how much it hurts others when he is unkind with his words and actions. He has apologized and Joshua has forgiven him. Now the boys are friends because Eden and Cade helped them.

Psalm 40:8 NIV

"I desire to do your will, my God;
your law is within my heart."

Jehovah Tsidkenu –"The Lord Our Righteousness."

Little Dreamer, Ignite!

Can you find the hidden dove in the picture?
Have you ever given help to someone who needed it?
When have you been unkind?
What can you and your families do to help others in your community who are not being treated kindly?
Would you like to thank God for forgiving you when you've been unkind?

Little Veterinarian, Ignite!

Little Luke and Kate have travelled to a horse ranch today to help one of the horses give birth to her baby. When they arrive at Little Dreamer Ranch, Kate and Luke walk into the barn and find, to their surprise, that not one, but two mares are ready to give birth. Luke helps Snowflake have her foal while Kate helps Cupcake have hers. Kate and Luke are so excited to see two happy and healthy little babies! They name them Snowman and Sprinkles.

Genesis 1:25 NIV

God made the wild animals according to their kinds, the livestock according to their kinds, and all the creatures that move along the ground according to their kinds. And God saw that it was good.

Jehovah-Raah –"The Lord My Shepherd."

Little Dreamer, Ignite!

Can you find the hidden dove in the picture?
Which foal do you think is Snowman, and which is Sprinkles?
Can you name seven different animals? Which is your favorite?
How can you help to take care of God's animal kingdom?
Would you like to thank God for animals large and small?

Little Writer, Ignite!

Little Mack and Quinn love to make up stories about all kinds of things and Mommy loves to help them write down their stories in a special notebook. Today, they are writing a story about a pretend place called Dream Lake, and in the middle of the lake there is the most magical waterpark that you could ever Imagine, with waterslides that go on forever and ever and ever! After the most amazing day and as Quinn and Levi slip into their warm sleeping bags, ready to go to sleep, they can't help but feel excited about all the adventures they get to write about tomorrow.

Exodus 32:15-16 NIV

Moses turned and went down the mountain with the two tablets of the covenant law in his hands. They were inscribed on both sides, front and back. The tablets were the work of God; the writing was the writing of God, engraved on the tablets.

El Shaddai –"Lord God Almighty."

Little Dreamer, Ignite!

Can you find the hidden dove in the picture?
What is one of your favorite stories?
Do you like to read or write poems, stories, or songs?
Can you make up a little story using your imagination right now?
Would you like to thank God for making you so creative?

Little Actors, Ignite!

Little Nate and Shae love acting in plays! For this play, Shae has chosen the pink princess costume and a bow and arrow. Nate has picked the knight costume and a sword. In the play, they ride in on their mighty horses to save the King and Queen of Little Dreamer Castle from an evil dragon. Once the dragon is defeated, and the play is over, Shae and Nate take a bow, and the audience explodes with clapping and shouts of joy.

Psalm 37:4 NIV

"Take delight in the Lord, and he will give you the desires of your heart."

Or Ha' Olam- "Light of the World."

Little Dreamer, Ignite!

Can you find the hidden dove in the picture?
When you're playing, what do you pretend to be?
Can you make up a little play with someone?
Have you been in a play before, at school or church or at home?
Would you like to thank God for your imagination?

Little Athlete, Ignite!

Little Micah and Sadie have been out of bed since 6:00 AM, getting dressed and ready for a very exciting day of soccer. After a thrilling game of running and kicking, cheering and high-fiving, all the players that won, receive trophies with their names on them. Micah and Sadie can't stop smiling. It's been the best day ever!

Isaiah 40:31 NIV
"Those who hope in the LORD will renew their strength.
They will soar on wings like eagles; they will run and
not grow weary; they will walk and not be faint."

Jehovah Jireh –"The Lord Will Provide."

Little Dreamer, Ignite!

Can you find the hidden dove in the picture?
Would you like to learn to play some other sports?
Which sports have you tried?
Can you name five different sports? Which is your favorite?
Would you like to thank God for making you strong?

Little Scientist, Ignite!

Little Reed and Eve are conducting a very exciting science experiment. They are making a little volcano that acts just like a *real* volcano, except theirs won't get burning hot! Mom and Dad have helped them put baking soda inside the cone they built. When they add the vinegar to it, everything begins to fizzle, and foam starts spurting up and over the top of the cone! Wow! How cool! shout Eve and Reed. "That's SO much fun!"

Psalms 111:2 NASB

Great are the works of the LORD; *They are*
studied by all who delight in them.

Alpha and Omega-"The Beginning and the End."

Little Dreamer, Ignite!

Can you find the hidden dove in the picture?
Do you know how scientists work with plants, animals, outer space, and medicine?
What kind of experiments have you done?
Can you name some tools used by scientists?
Would you like to thank God, for all the different ways science has helped you and your family?

Hidden Treasures in the Little Dreamer

Here are some of the characteristics often associated with the careers and callings we've just encountered. Do you see your Little Dreamer in the descriptions that follow? If so, pray, dream, and work toward helping your Little Dreamer engage in the world in ways that will ignite those God-given treasures. They very well may be tiny peeks into the beautiful plan God has for your Little Dreamer's future. Think outside the box! If, for example, your Little Dreamer is drawn to a police officer, you may support that learning and also plant ideas of other careers that require similar qualities and traits, such as fire fighters, other first responders, social workers, volunteers, the military, and many others. What sort of field trips, special outings, service projects, or visits with friends and loved ones at their workplaces could you enjoy with your Little Dreamers to expand their interests and experiences? Ignite!

Proverbs 22:6 NASB
Train up a child in the way he should go,
Even when he grows older, he will not abandon it.

Little Musician, ignite!

Characteristics of a Musician

Authentic, Dedicated, Creative, Passionate, Warm, Brave, Uniqueness, Compelled, Transparent, Driven, Complex, Persistent, Intelligent, Poetic, Independent

Little Doctor, Ignite!

Characteristics of a Doctor

Innovative, Compassionate, Hardworking, Confident, Scholarly, Realistic, Honest, Contemplative, Organized, Curious, Dedicated, Stable, Disciplined, Selfless, Empathetic, Focused, Generous, Healthy, Heroic, Honorable, Intelligent, Observant, Passionate, Considerate, Sympathetic

Little Teacher, Ignite!

Characteristics of a Teacher

Determined, Adaptable, Caring, Compassionate, Persistent, Creative, Intelligent, Cooperative, Dedicated, Empathetic, Engaging, Forgiving, Generous, Inspirational, Kind, Organized, Passionate, Patient, Resilient, Resourceful, Trustworthy, Responsible, Hard working, Selfless

Little Dancer, Ignite!

Characteristics of a Dancer

Collaborative, Passionate, Physically strong, Athletic, Hard working, Dedicated, Driven, Disciplined, Persistent, Energetic, Creative, Focused, Innovative, Intelligent

Little Police Officer, Ignite!

Characteristics of a Policeman

Ethical, Loyal, Justice driven, Patriotic, Hard working, Community focused, Dedicated, Fearless, Heroic, Generous, Intelligent, Street-smart, Observant, Respectful, Caring, Kind, Tireless, Mindful, Honest, Courageous, Selfless, Brave

Little Astronaut, Ignite!

Characteristics of an Astronaut

Courageous, Scholarly, Adaptable, Mentally durable, Strong, Intelligent, Dedicated, Innovative, Competitive, Adventurous, Confident, High-achieving, Committed

Little Lawyer, Ignite!

Characteristics of a Lawyer

Analytical, Studious, Discerning, Skilled in communication, Creative, Strong interpersonal skills, Logical, Justice-driven, Persevering, Persuasive, Intelligent, Wise, Relational, Empathetic, Compassionate, Sympathetic

Little Veterinarian, Ignite!

Characteristics of a Veterinarian

Compassionate, Animal-loving, Dedicated, Intelligent, Engaging, Innovative, Healing, Skilled in communication, Trusting, Dynamic, Honorable, Disciplined, Tireless, Kind, Responsible, Passionate, Empathetic

Little Writer, Ignite!

Characteristics of a Writer

Imaginative, Creative, Highly literate, Adventurous, Insightful, Thoughtful, Disciplined, Intelligent, Patient, Ambitious, Tough, Organized, Driven, Competent, Contemplative, Honest, Scholarly

Little Actor, Ignite!

Characteristics of an Actor

Captivating, Confident, Creative, Driven, Curious, Playful, Demonstrative, Intelligent, Charismatic, Professional, Reliable, Prepared, Determined, Imaginative, Flexible, Dedicated

Little Athlete, Ignite!

Characteristics of an Athlete

Dedicated, Mature, Disciplined, Driven, Professional, Passionate, Dreamer, Competitive, Insistent, Focused, Agile, Committed, Determined, Tolerant, Relentless, Physically fit

Little Scientist, Ignite!

Characteristics of a Scientist

Observant, Curious, Logical, Creative, Skeptical, Objective, Resourceful, Thinks outside of the box, Intelligent, Persistent, Analytical, Innovative, Passionate, Dedicated

Little Dreamer Treasure Hunt

Use the following pages to write the names of your Little Dreamers and all the embers of possibility you've unearthed within them while on your treasure hunt together. Pray about and record the ways you intend to fan the flames. Consider the depth and beauty of God in the stories He is writing in your Little Dreamers' lives—and your own. Write down your hopes and dreams for your Little Dreamers as they venture out into the promising futures Abba Father has prepared for them. There is one page for each of your Little Dreamers—and please don't miss the prayer at the end of the book.

Ephesians 2:10 NIV
"For we are God's handiwork, created in Christ Jesus to do good
works, which God prepared in advance for us to do."

Little Dreamer _____, *Ignite!*

Psalm 127:3 CEV
Children are a blessing and a gift from the LORD.

Little Dreamer _____, *Ignite!*

Deuteronomy 30:6 NLT
"The LORD your God will change your heart and the hearts of all your descendants,
so that you will love him with all your heart and soul so you may live."

Isaiah 54:13 NIV
"All your children will be taught by the
Lord, and great will be their peace."

Little Dreamer _____, *Ignite!*

Psalm 115:14 NLT
"May the LORD richly bless both you and your children."

Little Dreamer _____, *Ignite!*

Deuteronomy 29:29 NIV

"The secret things belong to the LORD our God, but the things revealed belong to us and to our children forever, that we may follow all the words of this law."

A Prayer to Pray Over Your Little Dreamers

Dear Abba Father,

I pray that _____ whom you have called by name, will know that you have a hope and a future for them-a purpose that is brighter and fuller than their little hearts could imagine. May these Little Dreamers walk out confidently in the fullness of all you have created them to be.

May _____'s dreams be ignited in beautiful new ways, and may they know deep and sweet intimacy with you, personally experiencing your great love for them.

May _____'s stories be filled with the richness of the heavens, and may your presence be their constant comfort and source of life.

May those who love these Little Dreamers always cherish the adventures that these little ones are on.

Thank you, Father, for pursuing us relentlessly. Thank you for the privilege of seeking out the jewels you have placed in all of us. Thank you that each and every child is a promise from your heart to ours.

Amen!

Printed in the United States
by Baker & Taylor Publisher Services